This Little Tiger
book belongs to:

_____

_____

_____

For Marianne, Bo, Claire, Liv and Luna,
with all my love – R G

LITTLE TIGER PRESS
1 The Coda Centre, 189 Munster Road,
London SW6 6AW
www.littletigerpress.com

First published in Great Britain 2013
This edition published 2013

Text and illustrations copyright © Ruth Galloway 2013
Ruth Galloway has asserted her right to be
identified as the author and illustrator of this work
under the Copyright, Designs and Patents Act, 1988

A CIP catalogue record for this book is available
from the British Library

ISBN 978-1-84895-544-8
Printed in China
LTP/1400/0496/1112

2 4 6 8 10 9 7 5 3 1

Smiley Shark

and the Great BIG HiCCuP!

Ruth Galloway

LITTLE TIGER PRESS
London

Far away, in the deep rolling ocean,
the fish were all in a frenzy.
Smiley Shark had disappeared!
"Whoohoo, Smiley Shark! Where
are you?" called Angelfish.

The friends searched in the swirling seaweed and around the colourful coral, but they couldn't find him anywhere!

At last, Octopus spotted him, but poor
Smiley Shark had lost his smile!

"What's wrong, Smiley Shark?"
asked Starfish.

"I can't **HiC** get rid of these annoying **HiC** hiccups!" Smiley Shark grumbled.

"I know what to do!" cried Angelfish. "When I have hiccups I swim as FAST as I can. That ALWAYS makes them go."

With a swoosh and a whoosh,
Smiley Shark and Angelfish
whizzed off as fast as
they could swim.

But it didn't work!

"Oh please, Starfish, **Hic** can you **Hic** help me?" asked Smiley Shark.

"Of course!" smiled Starfish. "When I have hiccups I do CARTWHEELS and that ALWAYS makes them go."

HIC!

whooooOOOOOO!

With a swish and a swirl they tumbled
and twirled together across the sand.

But that didn't work either!

HiCCuP! HiCCuP!

Smiley Shark was feeling very dizzy
AND he still had the hiccups!
"I have an idea," said Octopus.
He slowly reached out with his
twisty, tickly tentacles . . .

and tickled Smiley Shark
on the tummy.

Smiley Shark wriggled and
giggled and jumped and jiggled.
But it didn't stop his hiccups!

"I know just what will work,"
cried Pufferfish. "When I have hiccups, I hold
my breath for as LONG as I can and
that ALWAYS makes them go."

They both took a big gulp of water
and counted 1, 2, 3 . . .

"…HOORAY!
My hiccups have gone!"
grinned Smiley Shark.
"Thank you so much,
Puffer-HIC HIC HIC!"

Smiley Shark's hiccups were back,
and they were worse than ever!
His tummy jumped and bumped,
and span and twirled . . .

HiC!

HiC!

HiiiiiiCUP!

Poor Smiley Shark was getting very grumpy and grumbly. "I'll NEVER get rid of these **Hic** annoying hiccups!" he wailed.

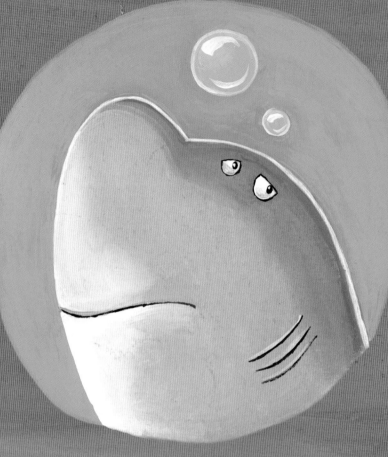

"We need a better plan," Starfish suggested. The friends huddled together and whispered.

Then Angelfish said with a smile, "Why don't you swim to the back of Big Coral Cave. You'll definitely find the cure for hiccups there!" "Really?" cried Smiley Shark. Determined to try, he swam off, still hiccupping gently.

HiC! HiC! HiC!

Inside the cave it was dark and rather lonely.
Bravely, Smiley Shark waited . . .

HiC! HiC! HiC!

"BOO

The scary surprise chased Smiley Shark's hiccups away!
"HOORAY!" he cheered. "Now we can all play
together! Thank you, everyone!"

"... **HiC!**" said Pufferfish.

Little Tiger books to make you giggle!

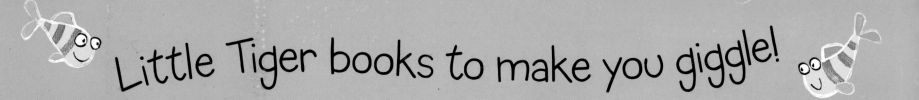

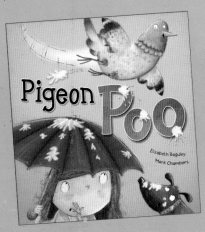

Pigeon Poo

Elizabeth Baguley
Mark Chambers

Steve Smallman · Hannah George

Dr Duck

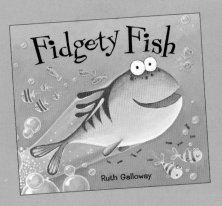

Fidgety Fish

Ruth Galloway

with fold-out pages

MY MONSTER DUMPER TRUCK

Steve Smallman · Joelle Dreidemy

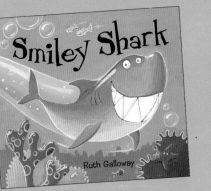

Smiley Shark

Ruth Galloway

A NEW Lazy Ladybird Adventure

Look Out, Ladybird!

Jack Tickle

For information regarding any of the above titles or for our catalogue, please contact us:
Little Tiger Press, 1 The Coda Centre, 189 Munster Road, London SW6 6AW
Tel: 020 7385 6333 • Fax: 020 7385 7333
E-mail: info@littletiger.co.uk • www.littletigerpress.com